21st Century Skills **INNOVATION** *Library*

Television

by Michael Teitelbaum

INNOVATION IN ENTERTAINMENT

![Cherry Lake Publishing]

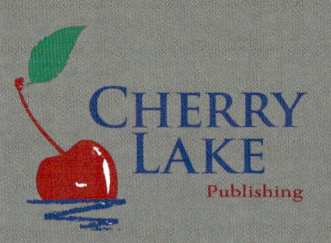

Published in the United States of America by Cherry Lake Publishing
Ann Arbor, Michigan
www.cherrylakepublishing.com

Content Adviser: Michael Niederman, Television Chair, Columbia College Chicago

Design: The Design Lab

Photo Credits: Cover and page 3, ©Horizon International Images Limited/Alamy; pages 4 and 15, ©ClassicStock/Alamy; page 6, ©Mary Evans Picture Library/Alamy; pages 9 and 17, ©AP Photo; page 12, ©iStockphoto.com/PaZo; page 13, ©Ronen, used under license from Shutterstock, Inc.; page 14, ©iStockphoto.com/slinscot; page 18, ©The Print Collector/Alamy; page 21, ©Photo Japan/Alamy; page 22, ©Kevin Foy/Alamy; page 24, ©Photo by: NBCU Photo Bank via AP Images; page 27, ©Boitano Photography/Alamy; page 29, ©Photos 12/Alamy

Copyright ©2009 by Cherry Lake Publishing
All rights reserved. No part of this book may be reproduced or utilized in any form or by any means without written permission from the publisher.

Library of Congress Cataloging-in-Publication Data
Teitelbaum, Michael.
 Television / By Michael Teitelbaum.
  p. cm.–(Innovation in entertainment)
 Includes index.
 ISBN-13: 978-1-60279-263-0
 ISBN-10: 1-60279-263-1
 1. Television broadcasting–Juvenile literature. 2. Television–Juvenile literature. I. Title. II. Series.
 PN1992.57.T45 2009
 384.55–dc22   2008002034

Cherry Lake Publishing would like to acknowledge the work of
The Partnership for 21st Century Skills.
Please visit www.21stcenturyskills.org for more information.

CONTENTS

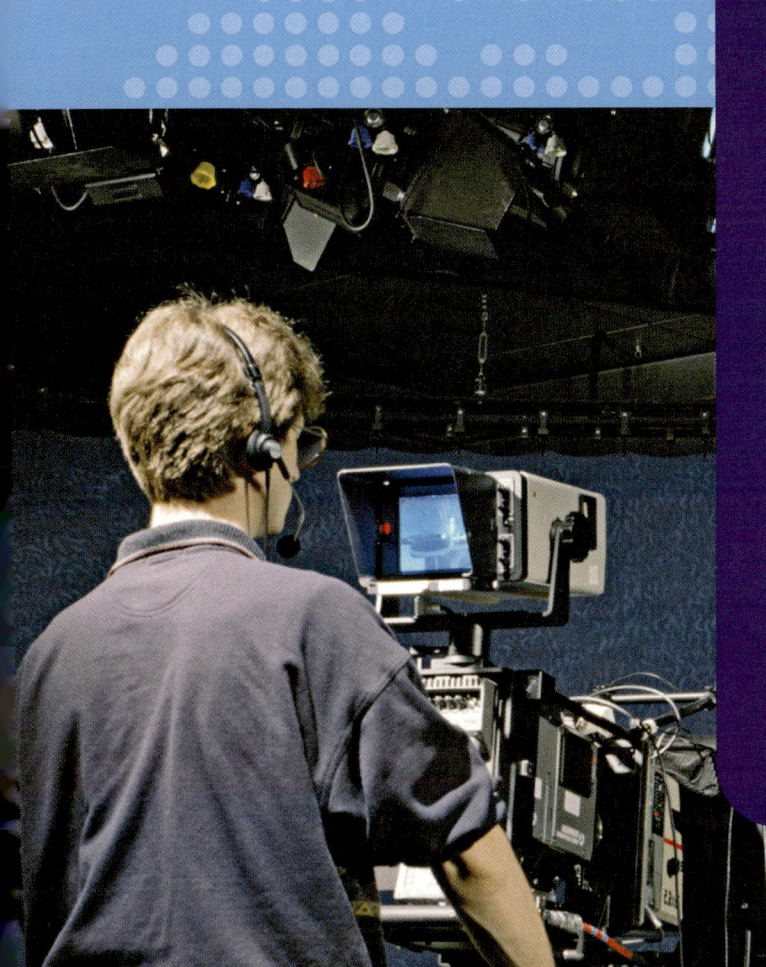

Chapter One
From Telegraph to Television   4

Chapter Two
Inventing Television   8

Chapter Three
Inform, Entertain, Advertise   13

Chapter Four
The Business of Television   21

Chapter Five
Some Famous Innovators   24

Glossary   30
For More Information   31
Index   32
About the Author   32

INNOVATION IN ENTERTAINMENT

CHAPTER ONE

From Telegraph to Television

Televisions of the 1940s and 1950s didn't look much like today's televisions. One thing that has stayed the same, though, is that many families still enjoy watching programs together.

The family gathered around the flickering box. Images of people and faraway places suddenly leapt right into their home. Movie stars, world champion athletes, and political leaders from every corner of the globe joined the family, entertaining and informing them.

Magic? Not really. Simply the magic of the invention we call television. But where did television come from?

❋ ❋ ❋

It started with the telegraph. Samuel F. B. Morse invented and developed this system for sending messages in the 1830s and 1840s. Before then, messages were sent from one place to another using signal flags or fires. Or someone had to physically deliver messages on foot or horseback. The telegraph allowed messages, in the form of beeping sounds, to travel long distances. The messages passed through wires.

Next came the telephone, invented by Alexander Graham Bell in 1876. This allowed the human voice to travel long distances, also through wires.

Then came the wireless telegraph, followed by radio. At first, radio was simply a wireless version of the telegraph. It was used as a way to get a message from one point to another.

But what if someone wanted to communicate with many people at the same time? It took the creative thinking of a **visionary** named David Sarnoff to change the way the technology was used. Sarnoff imagined using radio technology to send voices and music from one place to many places at the same time.

His idea caught on. By the 1920s, radio had taken over the country. The age of mass communication and mass entertainment had arrived.

After radios became popular, Sarnoff began to think about what would come next. At the 1939 World's Fair, he introduced a new invention called television. Sarnoff saw the potential of the device. He said that television would provide entertainment and information. Both sound and pictures would be beamed directly into homes.

At first, television broadcasts were few and far between. Not many people owned television sets. In 1940, there were only a few thousand TVs in use in the United States. Radios were still more popular. Eighty percent of homes had a radio at that time. But by the mid-1940s, the country had 23 television stations and more were on the way.

Bob Hope was one of television's most successful performers. He died in 2003.

From Telegraph to Television **7**

Many early television shows were based on existing radio shows. News, sports, quiz shows, comedies, and variety shows all appeared. Then, in 1948, a comedian named Milton Berle began hosting a variety show called *Texaco Star Theater*. It was the first "must see" television show in history.

By 1949, there were 1 million television sets in use in the United States. And that number was quickly growing. Actors such as Lucille Ball and Bob Hope became television stars.

The 1950s brought the development of television networks. These networks linked hundreds of television stations around the country. By 1955, more than half of the homes in the United States had TV sets. By the end of the decade, television had replaced radio as the main medium for home entertainment and information.

And it all began with the dots, dashes, and wires of the telegraph.

Learning & Innovation Skills

By 1927, a man named Herbert Ives had developed a method of transmitting television signals over long distances. He convinced Herbert Hoover, who was running for U.S. president, to appear on the system. Hoover was responsive to new ideas, and he became the first politician in history to appear on TV. Today, television is an important communication tool for politicians.

How do you think seeing a politician on TV can **influence** your opinion of him or her?

INNOVATION IN ENTERTAINMENT

CHAPTER TWO

Inventing Television

The idea for television was around long before the technology existed to make it a reality. In the early 20th century, science-fiction writers and cartoonists imagined a device that could beam pictures and sound from one place to another.

It wasn't just one person who created all the equipment needed to make television happen. Many scientists and engineers around the world built upon the work of those who came before them.

The technological road to television began back in 1884. That is when a German research student named Paul Nipkow created a mechanical form of television called the Nipkow Disc. Discs spun in both a camera and a receiver. Light passing through the discs created simple images.

Inventing Television

Vladimir Zworykin (left) receives an award for a scientific achievement in 1957. He is an important figure in the development of TV technology.

In 1897, a German physicist named Karl Braun invented the cathode-ray tube. When a beam of electricity in the tube hit a **fluorescent** screen, the screen glowed with an image. With this invention, television began evolving from a mechanical device to an electronic one.

Russian physicist Boris Rosing had an idea in 1907. He took Nipkow's two-disc sending and receiving system and replaced the receiving disc with a cathode-ray tube. Scottish engineer Campbell Swinton took Rosing's idea one step further. He proposed the first all-electronic television system. It would use cathode-ray tubes inside the TV camera that sent the picture. It would also use them inside the receiver that picked up the image. These ideas formed the early basis for modern television broadcasting.

Swinton's theories and ideas were put into practice in 1923 by Vladimir Zworykin. This Russian-born American engineer called his invention the iconoscope. This device became the heart of what evolved into the modern-day television camera.

Zworykin's work came to the attention of David Sarnoff. Sarnoff hired him to develop television for the company Sarnoff ran, RCA (Radio Corporation of America).

At this same time, a young, unknown American inventor was working on creating his own television system. His name was Philo Farnsworth. In 1928, he completed a working television system. Although Farnsworth doesn't get much credit for his work, many historians consider him to be the true father of television. His work, along with Zworykin's, helped finally make television a reality.

From the 1940s on, television technology went through many changes. But each change was a **refinement** or improvement upon what was already a working system. People wanted to keep making televisions that worked better and better.

For example, televisions only showed black-and-white pictures for years. The 1960s brought color television into the home. Color greatly enhanced the viewing experience. In the 1970s, cable television became popular. This not only delivered a cleaner, sharper picture but led to the rise of many new networks and programs. With cable, people had more shows to choose from.

In the 1980s, the home VCR (videocassette recorder) allowed viewers to record programs. They could then watch them later or more than once. Timers allowed viewers to tape programs even

Learning & Innovation Skills

From the very beginning, television pictures have been made up of a series of lines. The more lines, the clearer the picture. In 1928, the picture in Philo Farnsworth's television demonstration was made up of 60 lines. By today's standards, the picture wasn't very clear. But it was a starting point.

For many years, television sets used 525 lines. Today's high-definition televisions generate up to 1,080 lines of **resolution**. That sure is a clear picture!

Improving a product involves identifying what works well and what should work better. The process may include asking questions: Why doesn't something work? How can it be improved? Often, teams of experts must work through these questions together. What are some other questions to ask when improving a product?

INNOVATION IN ENTERTAINMENT

The invention of the home videocassette recorder (VCR) allowed viewers to record television shows to watch later.

when they were not home. People could watch their favorite shows whenever they wanted.

The late 1990s brought digital signals and high-definition television sets. This greatly improved the quality of the broadcast image. The new millennium introduced us to the digital video recorder (DVR). Like the VCR, the DVR allows viewers to record programs for later viewing.

The most recent technical developments in television have brought TV shows to our cell phones and laptops. But for now, at least, the most common way of watching shows is still on a television set.

CHAPTER THREE

Inform, Entertain, Advertise

Television's three main uses have always been to inform, to entertain, and to sell things. Almost since the birth of television broadcasting, advertisers were there. Advertisers paid for programs, just as they had for many years on radio.

Television looked to other media for program ideas. By the 1940s, radio offered a variety of programs. Comedy shows, dramatic shows, variety

Satellite dishes make it easier than ever to watch television programs from around the world.

INNOVATION IN ENTERTAINMENT

musical shows, quiz shows, and game shows all made the jump to television.

Early television broadcasts included live theatrical performances such as operas. Movies from the 1930s were also shown on television. This brought big-screen entertainment into the home for the first time.

Sporting events of all kinds and at all levels are popular with television viewers.

Walter Cronkite was one of television's most popular journalists.

Live sporting events were shown as well. These included boxing matches and college basketball games. In 1939, a Major League Baseball game was shown on television for the first time.

Television networks also worked to keep the public informed with nightly news broadcasts. They broadcast special coverage of important events, including the Republican and Democratic National **Conventions** in 1940.

In the 1950s, television truly became the **mainstream** home entertainment medium in the United States. The number of TV sets bought by consumers grew tremendously. The people who ran the television industry increased the number of stations and programs being broadcast. As consumers saw more stations and programs being made available, they became more comfortable buying TV sets of their own. They came to realize that this invention was not some gimmick that would vanish in a few months or years. Television was here to stay.

Television's main innovation was how it changed the way people received information, entertainment, and advertising in their homes. But the arrival of television also had a social and political effect on American society.

In the 1950s, for the first time, people all across the United States shared important moments through television. The full impact of television on politics became clear during the 1960 presidential election. John F. Kennedy's debates with Richard M. Nixon made Americans aware of the power of television to influence their lives.

Kennedy was young, handsome, and comfortable in front of the television cameras. Nixon was a far more experienced politician. But he sweated under the hot lights and appeared nervous and uncomfortable. Most people who watched the debates on television believed that Kennedy had won. But those who listened to the very same debates on radio believed that Nixon had won.

Inform, Entertain, Advertise   **17**

John F. Kennedy (right) appeared more comfortable than Richard M. Nixon (left) during their televised debates in 1960. Many people believe that this helped him win the election.

Seeing a confident Kennedy on television seems to have swayed some in his favor. Kennedy won the election by the narrowest of margins.

Americans have consistently turned to television for information and comfort during times of national tragedy. One such time was during the terrorist attacks of September 11, 2001.

Television has also been there during times of great achievement. Americans all watched together in

INNOVATION IN   ENTERTAINMENT

amazement when Neil Armstrong walked on the moon in 1969. The astronauts sent back live images from the moon's surface and gave us our first glimpse of Earth in space.

Television also exposed people to the realities of war. Night after night, the horror of young Americans fighting in the Vietnam War was beamed into American homes.

Millions of people tuned in to see man's first steps on the moon in 1969. This image shows astronauts Neil Armstrong and Buzz Aldrin unfurling a U.S. flag on the moon.

Several historians credit television with many Americans' growing awareness of and opposition to the war.

As television grew, it forced a change in the types of programming on radio. Talk and music took over the radio airwaves, leaving the comedies, dramas, and variety shows to TV.

Television's creative development is linked to its technical evolutions. For example, news, sports, and political coverage expanded when communications satellites were launched into space. They enabled networks to provide information from every corner of the world.

Television also grew as a storytelling medium. Early shows were shot inside studios. Even outdoor scenes were shot on sections of the studios' property called back lots. By the 1960s, TV dramas began to be shot on location. Different cities or remote parts of the world were used as their backdrops.

The subject matter of TV shows also grew up. Shows such as *All in the Family* in the 1970s tackled social, racial, and political issues that would have been unthinkable on TV just a few years earlier. A few decades later, HBO began producing shows such as *The Sopranos* and *Six Feet Under*. These shows were clearly aimed at adult viewers. They had a very high level of writing and acting, usually only found in feature films.

Life & Career Skills

In the early days of television, all shows were done live. This was before the invention of videotape. But by 1975, live shows were rare. That year, a new live comedy show called *Saturday Night* came onto the scene. It is now known as *Saturday Night Live*.

Performing on live television presents special challenges for actors. If they make a mistake, there's no starting over. Actors on live programs must work extra hard. That means being punctual and making the most of their time during rehearsal. It also means working well with other actors. After all, the actors in a scene are a team. And that team shares a common goal: a great performance.

The growth of the personal computer led to many new uses for television. Videoconferencing allowed people in different cities to attend the same meeting. It also opened up virtual field trips. Students could gather around a video monitor and tour a great museum halfway around the world.

Television is now used as a security tool, too. One person sitting in front of a group of TV screens can watch what is happening in many places at once.

Television has also become an important tool in the world of medicine. Doctors can now insert a tiny TV camera into a human body. They view the resulting images on a television screen.

In the span of a few decades, television has truly become a central part of our everyday lives.

CHAPTER FOUR

The Business of Television

The business of television is all about selling airtime to advertisers. Through television, companies with a product to sell can reach millions of people at once. This is also true with radio, but the addition of pictures gives commercials much more impact. Aren't you more likely to buy a product if you can see it, and not just hear about it?

David Sarnoff, the innovator who first imagined television as a household device, also came up with the idea for a television network. A TV network is a collection of many

Some companies advertise their products on giant television screens on the sides of buildings. This screen is in Tokyo, Japan.

INNOVATION IN ENTERTAINMENT

stations all over the country. They all broadcast the same programs and run the same ads.

RCA, Sarnoff's company, started NBC (National Broadcasting Company) in 1926 as a radio network. In 1939, Sarnoff formed the NBC television network. For advertisers, this new idea was great. Television networks allowed them to reach many more viewers than if they had to sell their ads station by station.

NBC's biggest competitor was CBS (Columbia Broadcasting System). Its head, William S. Paley, ran the CBS radio network. By 1941, he began moving his network into television.

Changes in technology also led to changes in the way television did business. Because advertisers paid for airtime, shows on basic television were presented for free.

NBC's logo is a colorful peacock.

With cable TV, the concept was that people would pay to have the television signal delivered to their homes over a wire. Many cable networks do not run commercials, though over the years, more and more have started to do so.

Digital technology arrived in the 1990s. With this technology, "pay-per-view" and "programs on demand" grew in popularity. Viewers are able to select and buy a TV show, movie, concert, or sporting event.

The Internet and cellular technology have also changed the way television does business. Viewers can download programs online and even watch them on their cell phones. Advertisers are constantly trying to come up with new ways to advertise their products. That can be a challenge because the medium of television keeps evolving.

21st Century Content

Have you ever noticed that many DVDs can be played in more than one language? Many people use DVDs and television as tools to help them learn another language. If you wanted, you could first watch your favorite movie in English. Then you could see it again in another language, such as French.

At any given moment, there's a good chance that someone somewhere in the world is watching a DVD. Companies realize this. By offering a greater variety of films to choose from, they have helped make DVD sales and rentals a multibillion-dollar global industry.

Online video rental companies make it easier than ever to find movies from other countries. What do you think you can learn about a different culture by watching a DVD from another country?

CHAPTER FIVE

Some Famous Innovators

David Sarnoff had many creative ideas for ways to use technology to bring entertainment into people's homes.

The contributions of many people have made television the popular and influential medium it is today. The list includes scientists, engineers, artists, and business experts. Here are just a few of television's most famous innovators.

David Sarnoff

If asked to pick the single most influential innovator in the development of television, many people would choose David Sarnoff. He rose to the top of the biggest communications company in the United States, RCA.

Sarnoff was a Russian immigrant who grew up poor. He learned **telegraphy** and was on duty the night the S.S. *Titanic* struck an iceberg. Using the telegraph, Sarnoff helped wire messages to other nearby ships. These communications helped save hundreds of lives that night. Following this event, wireless telegraph equipment became standard equipment on all large ships.

Many people thought wireless was only a means of emergency communication. But Sarnoff wanted to adapt the technology and apply it radio. He wanted to make it an entertainment medium. A few years later, he did the same thing with television.

Sarnoff also came up with the concept of a network. A network is a string of stations all connected by programming and advertising. The idea of the network helped make NBC a leader in the new medium.

Sarnoff ran the network until he retired in 1970. He died one year later.

Philo Farnsworth

Philo Farnsworth is considered by many to be the true father of television. He invented and built the first working, completely electronic television system. He revealed this system to the public in 1928. This was years before Sarnoff unveiled his television system at the 1939 World's Fair.

In 1919, Farnsworth was a teenager working on his family farm in Idaho. He read about Nipkow's mechanical television. As the story goes, he was out plowing fields one day. He looked out at the rows he had made and had a revolutionary idea. What if it was possible to **scan** a picture in the same way, one line at a time—as if you were reading a book?

Farnsworth's work was based on a straightforward concept. The idea was to turn pictures into lines, transmit this electronic information, and then turn the lines back into pictures. It remains the method used in televisions today.

Farnsworth didn't have the money available to him that Sarnoff had. He didn't have the scientists Sarnoff hired to develop electronic television for RCA, either. And so, although Farnsworth got there first, it was Sarnoff who first introduced television to America.

Farnsworth and Sarnoff battled in court for years, fighting over various **patents**. They disagreed about who should be given credit for inventing several of the technologies used in television. Unlike Sarnoff, Farnsworth never got rich from his invention.

Norman Lear was the most successful U.S. television producer of the 1970s.

Norman Lear

Norman Lear began creating television shows in the late 1950s. He will always be remembered for the groundbreaking shows he created in the 1970s. *All in the Family* dealt with social, political, racial, and generational issues. These kinds of issues had never been addressed before on American television. It was also one of the funniest and, at times, most touching shows ever broadcast. In shows such as *Sanford and Son*, *The Jeffersons*, *Maude*, and *One Day at a Time*, he created

Life & Career Skills

When people think of Lucille Ball, they think of one of television's funniest performers. But away from the camera, she was one of TV's shrewdest businesspeople and most innovative creators. Desilu was the company that she and her husband Desi Arnaz ran. It created several new methods of television production that are still used today. *I Love Lucy* was the first show to use three cameras to capture different shots and angles. Desilu also kept the rights to its shows. This allowed the company to make a lot of money selling the rights to rerun its shows to other television networks.

Ball was able to juggle the demands of two roles—entertainer and business owner—to succeed in all aspects of the television business.

unforgettable characters that quickly made viewers feel as if they were old friends. His shows made viewers think, laugh, and feel at the same time. Not an easy task for any TV program.

William S. Paley

William S. Paley is regarded as the innovator of the programming that went out over television's airwaves. Paley knew that the excitement surrounding the new invention of television would quickly wear off. He realized that if the networks did not provide quality programming, people would simply turn off their TV sets.

In the 1940s, Paley expanded the CBS radio network into television. It quickly overtook Sarnoff's NBC as the top TV network. His secret was to bring in the best talent. Journalists such as Walter Cronkite led his news department. Comedians such as

I Love Lucy, starring Lucille Ball (on right with husband Desi Arnaz), debuted in 1951. Reruns of the television comedy are still broadcast around the world in several languages.

Lucille Ball and Jackie Gleason created some of the most popular shows on TV.

Paley started airing children's programming with shows such as *Mr. I. Magination*. It was a science-based show that both kids and parents loved. And he introduced *The Ed Sullivan Show* in 1948. This variety program featured every top show business act for the next 23 years.

Paley helped define quality television for generations of TV viewers.

INNOVATION IN ENTERTAINMENT

Glossary

conventions (kuhn-VEN-chinz) large gatherings of people with the same interests or of the same political party

fluorescent (fluh-RESS-uhnt) giving off light when exposed to a certain kind of energy

influence (IN-floo-enss) to affect someone or something

mainstream (MAYN-streem) common or popular

patents (PAT-entss) legal documents that give only one person or group permission to make or sell an item

punctual (PUHNK-choo-uhl) on time

refinement (ri-FINE-ment) a change or improvement

resolution (rez-uh-LOO-shuhn) the clarity or sharpness of an image

scan (SKAN) to go over or examine in order to collect data

telegraphy (tuh-LEG-ruh-fee) the use of a telegraph to send messages

visionary (VIZH-uh-nair-ee) a person who imagines what will be possible in the future

For More Information

BOOKS

Raum, Elizabeth. *The History of the Television*. Chicago: Heinemann Library, 2008.

Richter, Joanne. *Inventing the Television*. New York: Crabtree Publishing Company, 2006.

Roberts, Russell. *Philo T. Farnsworth: The Life of Television's Forgotten Inventor*. Bear, DE: Mitchell Lane Publishers, 2004.

WEB SITES

Federal Communications Commission: Historical Periods in Television Technology
www.fcc.gov/omd/history/tv/
Explore television's fascinating history, from its origins to the digital age

MZTV Museum of Television
www.mztv.com/mz.asp
Find facts on television's greatest pioneers and explore a detailed timeline of television history

The TIME 100: Philo Farnsworth
www.time.com/time/time100/scientist/profile/farnsworth.html
For more on television's forgotten inventor

Index

advertisers, 13, 16, 21, 22, 23, 25
All in the Family television program, 19, 27
Armstrong, Neil, 18
Arnaz, Desi, 28

back lots, 19
Ball, Lucille, 7, 28, 29
Bell, Alexander Graham, 5
Berle, Milton, 7
Braun, Karl, 9

cable television, 11, 19, 23
cameras, 9–10, 16, 20, 28
cathode-ray tubes, 9–10
CBS (Columbia Broadcasting System), 22, 28
cell phones, 12, 23
color, 11
commercials. *See* advertisers.
communication, 4–5, 7, 19, 23, 24–25
computers, 12, 20
Cronkite, Walter, 28

Desilu company, 28
digital television, 12, 23
DVDs (digital video discs), 23
DVRs (digital video recorders), 12

Ed Sullivan Show, 28

Farnsworth, Philo, 10, 11, 25–26

Gleason, Jackie, 29

HBO cable network, 19
high-definition televisions, 11, 12
history, 4–7, 8–12
Hoover, Herbert, 7
Hope, Bob, 7

iconoscopes, 10
I Love Lucy television program, 28
Internet, 23
Ives, Herbert, 7

Kennedy, John F., 16–17

languages, 23
laptop computers, 12
Lear, Norman, 27–28
live programs, 14, 15, 18, 20

medicine, 20
Morse, Samuel F. B., 4
movies, 14, 23
Mr. I. Magination television program, 29

NBC (National Broadcasting Company), 22, 25, 28
networks, 7, 11, 15, 21–22, 23, 25, 28
news broadcasts, 7, 15, 17, 19, 28
Nipkow Disc, 9
Nipkow, Paul, 9, 26
Nixon, Richard M., 16

"on-demand" programs, 23

Paley, William S., 22, 28–29
patents, 26
pay-per-view, 23
politics, 7, 15, 16–17, 19, 27
programs, 7, 11, 12, 13–15, 16, 19, 20, 22, 23, 25, 27–29

radio, 5, 6, 7, 13, 16, 19, 21, 22, 25, 28
RCA (Radio Corporation of America), 10, 22, 25, 26
rights, 28
Rosing, Boris, 10

Sarnoff, David, 5, 6, 10, 21, 22, 24–25, 26, 28
satellites, 19
Saturday Night Live television program, 20

science-fiction, 8
security, 20
September 11 terrorist attacks, 17
shows. *See* programs.
Six Feet Under television program, 19
The Sopranos television program, 19
sports, 7, 15, 19, 23
stations, 6, 7, 16, 21–22, 25
Swinton, Campbell, 10

telegraphy, 4, 5, 7, 25
telephones, 5
television sets, 6, 7, 11, 12, 15–16
Texaco Star Theater variety show, 7

VCRs (videocassette recorders), 11, 12
videoconferencing, 20
Vietnam War, 18–19
virtual field trips, 20

wireless telegraphy, 5, 25
World's Fair, 5, 26

Zworykin, Vladimir, 9–10

About the Author

Michael Teitelbaum has been a writer and editor of children's books and magazines for more than 25 years. In addition to his fiction work, with characters ranging from Garfield to Spider-Man, Michael's most recent nonfiction books include *Mountain Biking*, *Rock Climbing*, and *Skiing* for Cherry Lake. His latest work of fiction is *The Scary States of America*, published by Delacorte in 2007. Michael and his wife, Sheleigah, live in New York City.

Television